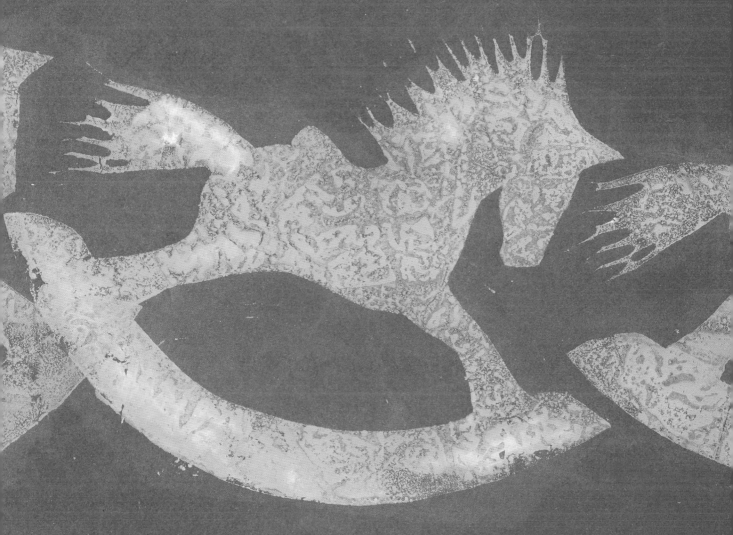

THE MAGIC SADDLE

THE
MAGIC
SADDLE

BY

CHRISTOBEL MATTINGLEY

ILLUSTRATED BY

PATRICIA MULLINS

Simon & Schuster Books for Young Readers

SIMON & SCHUSTER BOOKS FOR YOUNG READERS

An imprint of Simon & Schuster Children's Publishing Division

1230 Avenue of the Americas, New York, New York 10020

Originally published in Australia in 1983 by Hodder & Stoughton (Australia) Pty Limited.

Published in Australia in 1996 by Margaret Hamilton Books Pty Ltd.

First American Edition, 1996.

SIMON & SCHUSTER BOOKS FOR YOUNG READERS is a trademark of Simon & Schuster.

The text for this book is set in 13/18pt Palatino by Silver Hammer Graphics.

The illustrations are rendered in torn-tissue collage, lino block, crayon and watercolor.

Printed in Hong Kong.

10 9 8 7 6 5 4 3 2 1

ISBN 0-689-80959-X

Library of Congress Catalog Card Number 95-72230

For Stephen who believes that
books are magic saddles
and for Prudence who invites me on
her magic journeys

Jonni wanted a rocking horse. He wanted a rocking horse more than anything. But a rocking horse costs more than five pennies. And Jonni's parents were poor. And a rocking horse needs as much space as a bed. And Jonni's house was small.

In Jonni's little room high up under the rafters there was only space for his bed and his shoes. Jonni used to kneel on his bed and look out of his window, down at the town he knew so well and across to the mountains he did not know at all. And he wished for a rocking horse to take him away. Over the town and far away. Over the mountains and far, far away.

On Saint Nicholas' Day Jonni's parents took him to the Christmas fair in the marketplace. From his seat high up on his father's shoulders Jonni could see everything.

Over the tops of people's heads he could see popcorn popping, chestnuts roasting, and sausages cooking. He could see the brass band playing and the conjuror doing his tricks. He could even see Saint Nicholas himself.

They came to the toy stalls. Among the trumpets and the trains, the drums and the dolls, the tea sets and the teddy bears, the balls and the building blocks, Jonni saw a rocking horse. A rocking horse as large as life.

"I wish I could have that rocking horse," Jonni said.

His mother laughed. "You would have to keep it on the roof. There's no space in your room."

She dipped into a basket of tiny toys for hanging on a Christmas tree—bells, angels, snowmen, cuckoo clocks—and pulled out a little red rocking horse with a golden mane and tail. She paid the stallkeeper five silver coins and gave the red rocking horse to Jonni with a smile. "He's more your size. You can hang him on the wall above your bed."

Jonni thanked his mother and held the toy tightly. It was a dear little horse, its red rocker painted with white stars. But it was tiny. It could not carry him over the mountains and far away.

"I'm your horse too, Jonni," his father said. He gave Jonni the ends of his long scarf. "You only have to pull on the reins and I will take you wherever you want to go."

"Over the mountains and far away?" Jonni asked.

His father said, "Yes. It's time we went there."

And he carried Jonni through the crowd, over the tops of hats and parcels and sausages, to the big Christmas tree by the fountain.

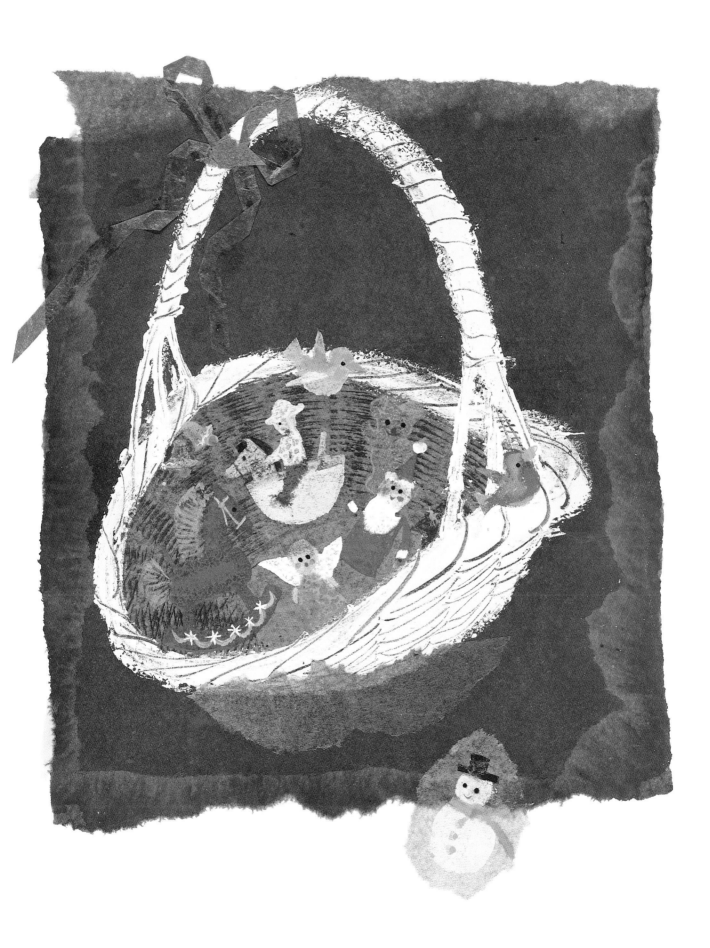

At the foot of the tree there was a crib, and the three kings were standing with the presents they had brought from far away—gold and frankincense and myrrh. They were very valuable presents, Jonni knew, but they were not for playing with. Jonni looked down at all the people crowding around the crib with their bags bulging with toys and presents for each other. But no one gave the Christ Child anything. And a little child must have a toy.

So, as his father turned away, Jonni leaned down and dropped the red rocking horse at the foot of the manger. It was just the right size for the Christ Child.

On Christmas Eve the Christ Child brought gifts for Jonni. There was a blue wool mouse with red ears and a long red tail, which fitted snugly in Jonni's pocket and felt cozy in his hand. There was a picture book of all sorts of animals from far-away places—monkeys and elephants, parrots and tigers.

And there was a rocking horse. A gingerbread rocking horse with currants for eyes, rockers decorated with cherries, and a saddle made of white icing.

Jonni was hungry. And what was the good of a gingerbread rocking horse, except for eating?

But his mother said, "You must brush your teeth now and go to bed."

So Jonni brushed his teeth and went to bed. And on his pillow was the picture book of animals and in his pocket was the mouse.

The gingerbread rocking horse was hanging on the window latch and Jonni lay staring at it in the starlight. If only it had been a real rocking horse . . . But what was the use of a gingerbread rocking horse?

He sat up. "You silly rocking horse! You are only gingerbread and I am going to eat you. First I will bite off your tail. Next I will eat your rockers. Then I will bite off your head. And last of all I will crunch up your saddle."

The rocking horse said, "It is true I am only gingerbread and you may eat me. But don't eat my saddle. It is a magic saddle and anyone who rides on it may go wherever he wishes."

Jonni asked, "Over the hills and far away?"

The gingerbread horse nodded and began to rock. The latch moved slowly and the window opened.

"Can we go now?" Jonni asked.

"Why not?" the rocking horse said.

At once Jonni was sitting on the magic saddle and the horse was rocking across the snowy rooftops, over the sleeping town, over the fields, over the forests, over the moonlit mountains, into the clouds.

On the other side of the clouds the sun was shining and the horse was rocking over sparkling blue sea. Jonni looked down on boats and whales and islands.

They reached a land where palm trees grew as tall as church towers, and the rocking horse came to rest. Some friendly monkeys threw down coconuts and Jonni had a long drink of sweet cool milk.

"I wish I were a monkey," the little mouse said, "so that I could bring you coconuts."

Jonni put his hand in his pocket and curled the mouse's tail around his finger. "I like you just as you are."

A friendly elephant brought Jonni a bunch of bananas.

"I wish I were an elephant," the rocking horse said, "so that I could bring you bananas. But you may eat some of my cherries if you are hungry."

"I like you just as you are," Jonni said. "And I wouldn't dream of eating any of your cherries."

Some friendly parrots flew by and called, "The tiger is coming!" Jonni saw stripey gold and black shadows under the palm trees.

"I like me just as I am," he said. "And I wouldn't dream of being eaten by a tiger!"

He hopped on the rocking horse very fast. And they rocked and rocked and rocked.

"Are you tired?" he asked the little rocking horse, when they arrived back at Jonni's attic window.

"No," said the rocking horse. "I am never tired. And I can take you anywhere you wish, whenever you want to go, on my magic saddle."

Jonni's father came in to check his bedcovers. It was very cold in Jonni's room, so his father brought his big coat and spread it over Jonni as he slept.

In the morning when Jonni woke, the animal book was by his pillow, the mouse was in his pocket, the gingerbread horse was hanging on the window latch, and the shoulders of his father's coat were humped around Jonni like a saddle.

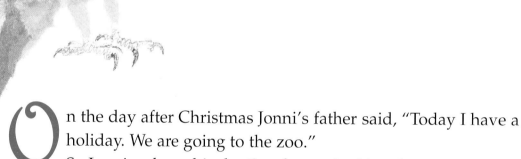

On the day after Christmas Jonni's father said, "Today I have a holiday. We are going to the zoo."

So Jonni rode on his daytime horse, looking down on monkeys and elephants and parrots. And when he saw the tiger he felt quite safe high on the saddle of his father's shoulders.

They had lunch in the palm house where it was warm and the palm trees grew almost as tall as church towers.

On the way home, Jonni's mother bought a coconut in the market. His father cut it and when they had eaten the sweet white flesh, Jonni hung the halves up by his window. One shell he put outside with crumbs for the birds which were not parrots. The other shell he put inside as a nest for the mouse who wanted to be a monkey.

And the rocking horse swung on the latch, ready to take Jonni wherever he wished, whenever he wanted to go.

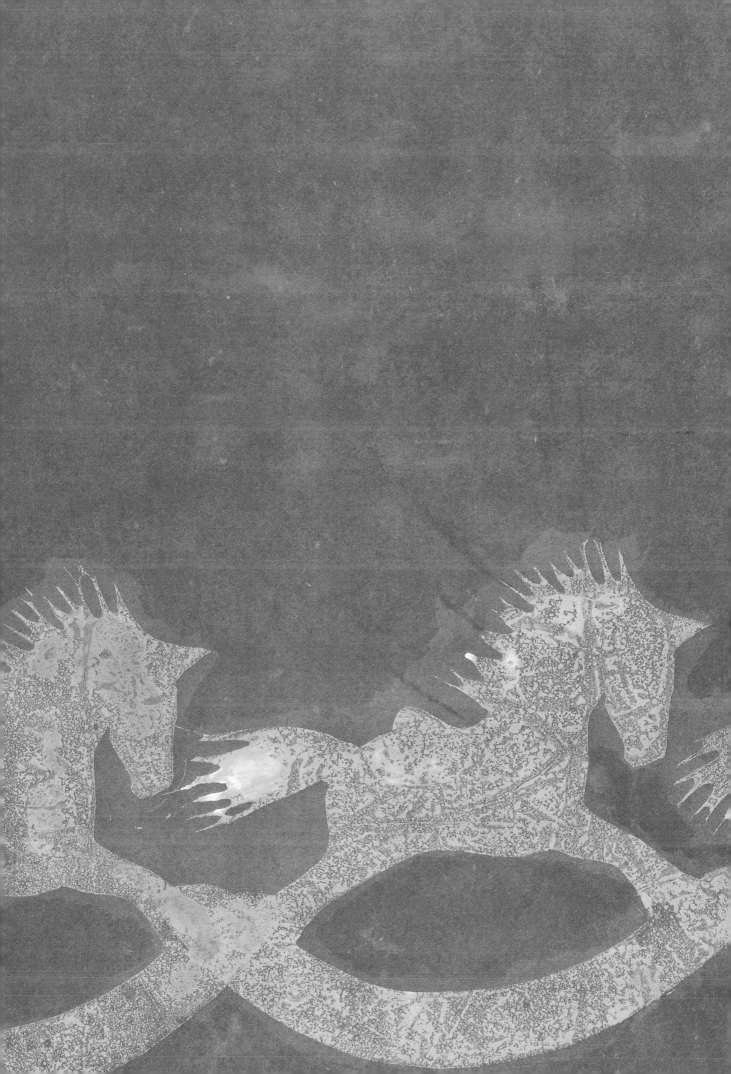